'ELVIS'ION

Poems of Tribute to Elvis Presley
by **Barbara Sherlow**
August 1977

First Published in Great Britain in 1999 by
Barbara Sherlow
'Libaral'
c/o Cremer Press

Printed and Bound by
Cremer Press
26 Whalley Banks
Blackburn BB2 1NU

Previous Titles by the same Author

Ho Ho Ho - Children Chuckles
Relative Values

CONTENTS

Title	Page

INTRODUCTION

The very sudden shock of the great Mister Elvis Presley rocked the world in 1977.

I hope my book of poems will help some of his very saddened fans.

I love to write poems.

This book is dedicated to all Elvis Fans everywhere. Cheer up Elvis Fans.

Supported by:
Preston Art Association

ELVIS'S FAVOURITE "LP"

"Princess" **L**isa **P**resley,
Daughter of the King,
For you he sang - "*Your Teddy-Bear*",
For your Mom - "*She Wears My Ring*"

Dark, handsome he, Elvis -
Mister Dynamite
Lisa, now *you're* chased, hounded, worried -
Forgive your Dad for your plight

Because *you* carry, the
Burden of Dad's fame,
You walk in his shadow girl, and
Share always his "Hallowed"name

Sorry to say li'l gal
People's blood is ice,
His popularity lives on,
You are left to pay the price

Little girl, your Daddy,
He lives on anew
The world's Elvis Presley told us
Lisa, it was all for you

Tho' your Dad is gone now,
Him no more you'll see -
But we know you are
Elvis' favourite **"LP"**.

ELVISION

I don't need to sleep Elvis
To dream of you -
Your vision follows me everywhere
In sleeping and daydreaming too!

For whichever way I turn
Your vision's there
Here in all of my "always" days where
You pass me on the stair!

In my thoughts and in my mind
In my study,
In my cassettes, records and CDs,
El, my star, my buddy

My aim is to stay loyal
I'm not debating,
King until I come to you
I'll be your "Lady-in-Waiting"

A guitar-strumming
Idol, always my revision
A handsome King
My ELVISION

To be a whole world's star was
EL's Vision
He made - oh - he made it - and how -
Mastered with precision!

God aimed and fired the "shot" and
Heaven targeted the wicket
Elvis we're pleased to know, oh yes,
You're on a first class ticket

With an eye on the past that's
Appearing now as a dot
A sad Elvis-less world and future
Now is all we got!

"Stay in my vision"

1

LEAVING HIS HEAVEN - FOR ANOTHER

A twelve-year-old foreign boy
Received a guitar for his birthday
Overjoyed with his gift
The guitar remained with him always

And this was the start of all
Swooning girls for this Spanish-type boy,
A world gone so crazy
With ecstatic love and extreme joy!

Swoonings, faintings, screamings, were,
A way of life that became "his trade",
Never been anything
To compare with the impact he made!

Was it Christopher Columbus who claimed
The world was round and all that?
Elvis I'd like to reverse that claim
And say - now - my world is flat!

BEGGAR-MAN TO A KING

Tho' you're gone
King Elvis Presley,
I shall go on looking up to you
Your Majesty

Not a wreath
Nor even prayer-book,
I placed a kiss in the flowers you'll find
There if you look

What is gold
And what are jewels?
Only mere trophies that cannot fight
Death's duels

Don't have much
But this Sev'nty Seven
I have helped to make another Star
For God's heaven

Only a farewell kiss
Can I bring
Wrapped in love Elvis from
Beggar-man to King.

PRESLEY ADDICT

I'll never know what he had
But he sure had it,
Every kid -
A Presley addict!

Sure he had drive, ambition,
But so had them all
So why just he
Always ten feet tall?

He appealed to all ages -
There's not many do
Who else'd do it
Come - I ask you - who?

Presley death, fun'ral - on earth,
"The greatest show"
Biggest idol
Since Valentino!

Teenagers view their dads - as "old"
Past forty, yes, it's in their page,
But suddenly *Elvis* dies - aged "forty-two"
and it's -
Fancy - he's left us - at such a *young* age.

HOW DEEP MY BLUE

I'm so much older now Elvis
Why d'ya do it?
I'm just not the same girl any more
Not one bit

I feel my heart sinking lower,
My cheeks are so pale,
And I look down at these hands of mine
They've gone frail!

You never sang a song
That could describe how deep my blue,
So right here and now
I'm writing one for you

If was granted one wish to me
It would be just this,
Save me a place right next to you
King Elvis

I'll never marry now, for you'll
Always be my man.
You will never learn of *me* now -
I'm just a fan.

THE REAL THING - THE REAL KING

Records, films, radio, TV,
Cannot replace
The real thing - the real King,
And his handsome face

Apple of everyone's eye, El
Was often kissed
Best of best - the fav'rite
Of impressionist

Try as you may all you Pop-Stars
To reach his height,
He "didn't want be a tiger"
But wondered
- "*Are you lonesome tonight?*"

"Great songs Elvis."

ELVIS PLEASURABLY

Exciting

Loving

Vivacious

Intoxicating

Soul-inspiring

Pleasing

Re-assuring

Ever-King

Sky-high stardom

Leisurely

Everlasting

Yippee!

- Elvis - Who Else?

TRIPLE-MEANING NAME

"Elvis let's live together!"
This forever was my dream
If you would grant me this,
So loud would be my scream!

Elvis let's sing together,
Record us in harmony
The label's all bearing,
"Presley - him'n' me!"

Your name re-arranged spells "Lives"
How can you be dead?
Re-arranged again spells "Lives" (eye)
All girls wished to you they're wed!

Elvis let's die together
There's nothing if you're not here
Never more to see you
In your sparking white gear!

Elvis let's return together
To the world - re-united!
Surely you hear its call
Oh how you are invited!

SORRY! - IF THERE'S SUCH A WORD

Sorry! - If there's such a word
For it is seldom heard
Seemed little meaning to it somehow
That is - up until now

Sorry! - The word sounds so meek
For it we seldom speak,
But only this word can express
"The" death - the awful mess!

Oh Elvis there's never been
A sorrier thing
To happen to this world,
Than to lose its King

Sorry! - Uttered on all lips,
Except in cautious slips
We speak it over and often
But the blow doesn't soften

Yet another
Sad state of affair,
Poor world must now live in sorrow
Elvis is no longer there.

GOD'S THE BEST JUDGE

Elvis you should never have allowed
The pressures to get a hold on you,
We'd've awaited your date

Elvis, surely you knew that we would
Definitely have pulled you through
When the pressure got too great!

God - He knew He had *to*
Take one adored
Oh it isn't right
To tempt the Lord!

You didn't properly tend your life
Sorry - but *you* put pressure on *Him*
Careful, He, with lives He gives

Elvis, God doesn't like misuse,
He looks upon this purely as sin,
We won't question His motives

Maybe He'll send
Another Angel to sing.
Heaven knows why -
God took our King!

ANGEL ELVIS

Shame on me - in a way,
Entering contests for a "King" prize,
Yes but his records are special
And may help to dry my eyes

To write words - is easy,
Much harder to mend this heart God broke
We should all have helped Elvis when
He announced - "It's time to talk"

For had we - slowed down then,
God may have taken strain from our King,
But caught up in our greedy web
He's now nevermore to sing!

In a poem such as this
Seems useless to sign with a kiss,
The eyes that view will not be his,
Goodnight, God Bliss,
Angel Elvis!

AMERICA'S KING

Long reign - short life
Is the story of Elvis
Creating Heaven on Earth
He was good at this

Not world riches
Go in making of King,
For in his very nature
There was everything!

Looks, confidence,
So way up until the end,
Fame, friends, and fans followed him -
America's legend!

Some loved "The Leg"
And some his song
- Whatever -
He could never go wrong!

ONE OF THE GREATS

You won't need to ask "Who?"
He was "one of the family"
His voice still in my ears
Cries "adios" to me

Now we're mourning Elvis,
One of the Greats,
King for America
Passes through the Pearly-Gates

Welcome him, this he's earned,
Now that his short life is all through
All ready in his white,
God, as he comes to you!

Yet living dangerously
And seemingly wildly,
To say he was famous
Is puting it mildly

Tho' his light is out now
Elvis's story still glows,
"Rock" him, only, now as
His book comes to a close!

BITTER SWEET YEAR

The year Nineteen-Seventy-Seven brought
A Queen's Jubilee to catch our breath,
But contained also, the tragic
Elvis Presley's death

God, how you've mixed up this so happy year,
One part we're happy, the next we grieve,
Frustrated now your happy world
Saddened by his leave!

Oh bitter-sweet year
Seventy-Seven,
You took a Queen - and a "King"
Right into a Heaven!

Elvis is gone now to *his* Heaven he
Bids us not to mourn him, but to sing
"All-the-Seven's-Year" - Joy for a Queen,
Sadness for a "King"

The Queen walked about
A tiny "hello" - a quiet word,
Then it came - the loudest goodbye
The world's ever heard

- Translation of above ...

- "Our Queen Elizabeth was taken
into a gigantic "Heaven" of joy
and happiness of her Jubilee"

HIS SPIRIT INSPIRES ME

Never to be forgotten
He made it too high
Elvis - he is not dead
A King does not die

Oh I am so privileged
The one in the land,
He pushes my pen
While he guides my hand

Right now as I write
His spirit inspires me,
And I can feel the nearness
Of Elvis Presley

I can't wait to be alone
That's when he's closest,
My Elvis, my King
I love the mostest!

I try try to carry on
But goodness El,
It's hard now you've left us
A foot in Heaven, and one in Hell!

NOW HE'S MINE

Poor Elvis could have done to be divided
For such a life had he,
The ladies charmingly exclaiming
"And he belongs to me"

Agents, fans, managers, how much could he take?
The whole world wanted him
With his shimmering shake
How could his life be dim?

Tho' God understood,
To his world Elvis was good,
Respectfully he said,
"You've had him a long time
Now He's mine."

Pity his twin brother could not have survived
He'd have maybe helped the load,
Our King might have lived on
- Elvis who Rock 'n' Rolled.

ELVIS PRESLEY

E is for the Kingdom carried on   Endlessly

L is for the way he did it quite   Leisurely

V says it all happened so   Visually

I for the one -   Inevitably

S imply -   Sorry

P is the dynamic   Personality

R we'll remember so   Rememberingly

E for songs he devoured   Edibly

S he lived quite   Singingly

L a chosen career he   Longingly

E respectfully he strove for   Eternally

Y the yearn now carried of his fans   Yearningly

Quiet now his songs
As we listen leisurely.
Long may he reign
Elvis - Elvis Presley.

17

LEAVING HIS WORLD

Leaving his world he's
Gone now to where *his* King waits,
Leaving his fans to mourn,
Gone now through those Pearly Gates

Rest comes at last for he whom
The whole world's eyes lit up for
For when Saint Peter knocked
He had to open the door

All ages
Under the Elvis spell,
Filled with empty loss,
Now he leaves his
"Heart-Break Hotel"

And so he leaves us
Here, where he was plenty "girled",
Leaving an emptiness
He's gone now to *his* King's world

Maybe now he's in spirit,
Maybe now he'll know I exist,
But even so Elvis -
Consider your lips kissed.

I DANCED WITH ELVIS

We all danced to your records last night
Elvis, I should have stayed home,
Your voice reaching up to the skies
And way down the microphone

It was bad enough hearing a Jive
But the "Smooch" was agony,
Then I glanced up at my partner
Could have sworn it was you dancing with me

We were surrounded by a Heaven,
My feet were tapping the boards
Elvis you were never so near -
A ghost 'n' me dancing to your records

After thirty-minutes
We were wading in the tears,
A memory in our hearts
You in our ears.

Written day after Tribute Dance held
at Wallys - 29 August 1977

(Wally Hobkirk's Dance Hall, Preston)

ELVIS IF YOU HEAR ME

Elvis King
You're gone somewhere,
Leaving us with
This cross to bear

Sorrow with
A world I share,
A dead guitar
A stage that's bare

Elvis if you hear me,
Carry on being dead;
But to me and millions
You've only gone to bed

Your picture
Each day, says "Please,
Why should you mourn
I've gone to peace"

I turn now
With a soft shout,
"Presley tickets -
Now sold out!"

FATHER OF THEM ALL

What a very quiet world now
It's "Kingless",
Long two-minute silences
For Elvis

He has stolen away to Jesus
A world's "Pop",
Who started at the bottom -
Died at the top

Many are the sons
Of Rock 'n' Roll,
But now we've lost
The "Father" of them all!

Often clad Cowboy style 'n all
In white suit,
Upset myself, I write this
My tribute

Should you drop in America,
Its sad band
Will be glad he's remembered
In England.

STRONG PAPER-CLIP

I can't stop writing tributes,
He's more powerful with each line;
It's gonna take a strong-paper-clip
To keep his life in mine!

As I'm writing now on paper,
I am shown his rascally wink;
"It's up to you now", he is saying,
"I'm holding fast the link!"

*My weaker heart cries
Elvis, now you're gone forever,
Gonna take a strong everything
To keep us together!*

Firmly holding back my tears,
Along with the rest I pine
For my precious Presley idol and
His hand is strong on mine.

GOD'S HONOURED GUEST

He didn't have to search you out,
For you stood Elvis as the best,
You're gone now as
God's honoured guest

A day started and ended with
You and your precious influence,
Taken from us
Doesn't make sense

Starting as a David,
Ending as Goliath,
When the Lord asks - "Who's missed him?"
I'll whisper - "I have"

Around thirty songs ago,
I could have sworn you mentioned me
Fancy - mentioned by -
Elvis Presley!

Now as you sit up there with God
Where the good angels kiss your shoe,
I wonder on
Who's honouring who?

ENTERTAINING ANGELS

You've got a brand new audience now
And they won't treat you rough,
One of a tranquil kind
And nowhere near as tough

For you are not dead to them, oh no
It's us have to be strong
We're the ones going to be
Minus you and your song!

Do your best for them as you did for us,
"Heavenly" now you sing
Peace'll be yours all the way
You are under their wing!

When your show begins Elvis, I know
You will earn their applause
An added tour for you
When unto God you rose!

You're entertaining angels now
Should I feel jealousy?
Yet I think not for I
Loved Elvis Presley!

PREFER DAYDREAMS TO NIGHTMARES

Elvis I had the most vivid nightmare
Last night in my bed
Oh Elvis the shock
I dreamt they told me you were dead

Oh I couldn't wait to waken today
To make sure how true,
And to my horror
The sad world had bad news of you

Elvis you have gone with the nightmare
You've taken your crown
I must carry on,
But seems you've let my daydreams down!

The newsmen thought
They were bearers
Of tragic news today,
But pipped at the post they
By my nightma-res

Oh I prefer daydreams to nightmares,
Ah yes any time
In a nightmare you are God's,
In a daydream you are mine!

HE WAS OURS

An ever-striving Elvis,
His way from the start was lit;
Without a "song-and-dance"
He made it

In the "steal" business he too,
For he sure stole hearts and lives,
All the single girls
And the wives!

In this stardom world
There have been hosts of stars,
But this one - he -
Was our's!

Popular yes - even now,
Now with his life all out;
He's good subject to
Write about

Ours - an extra quality
To keep among my "My's",
Down years there was *Our*
Star - King-size!

LIFE ON THE TURNTABLE

Elvis King Presley
Since the world became ill
Due to your passing
Our turntable's still

Left in a turmoil
I'm still on the round-a-bout
Giddy, dizzy,
From your death's shout

It was always you did the spinning
In our home,
Now the turntable
Stands there alone!

I know you'll "return"
As soon as you're able
For now - you're left
On the turntable

"When we come to terms with death
We come to terms with life too
Spin back into our lives
Elvis, the world is dead - not you!"

IF EVER THERE'D BEEN

If ever there'd been
A meeting 'tween you and I,
Elvis I'd've been a dummy
I would have been so shy

Now I can get
All the best things
Off my chest
Now you're at rest

If ever there's <u>been</u>
A man higher than a King,
Through these pages of *your* book's
History, Elvis I bring

If ever there's been
Any brighter "Score-Plus" years
That were spent for others -
Sadly - ending with tears

If ever there's been
A Devil enjoying
That crucial moment when
The Devil was employing.

FAV'RITE ANGEL

Where you're gone to Elvis
Maybe there'll be no special lights,
Maybe we can't blame God for your passing
God doesn't have favourites

But we want you to know
We've <u>sure</u> felt the pull,
I think I speak for a world when I say
You're our favourite angel

God's holding up His hand
"It isn't fair to use up tears,
This is not what pillows were made for",
And - "Hearts were meant for cheers"

And so with time to spare,
And to let you go I vow,
I bend my head in an Elvis prayer
Heart healed a little now!

"Life must flow with the tide
'Tis you must go, and I must bide."

ARE FLOWERS ENOUGH?

His jewels could not compare,
Nor his flashy cars,
With the other he had -
A deep love that was ours

I convey deepest sympathy,
But a load of "sloppy stuff"
Is not me - so -
Are flowers enough?

My bouquets are numerous,
Plenty my kisses
Sorry, world, but have to say
These are Elvis's!

The "Language-of-their-own" these flowers
Do talking for me,
My sitting-downs are restless,
My walking - stormy!

Peace only from the flowers
That comfort lonely hours.

GUIDE OUR LITTLE ONES

When all the rest are looking
From their window, what the weather will do
Elvis every morning
I am looking at you

And I remember from your picture
The electrifying "Presley bombs"
Into a self-same glory,
Elvis guide our little ones!

"Rock" them from the cradle
"Roll" *them* in a "Red Carpet" too
Elvis tho' you're not with us
We're relyin' on you!

They're trying to be just like you,
These kids already are copying
This is great but we do not
Want their lives sloppying!

Stay with them El,
Use your influence;
Only this, to them,
Will make any sense!

HISTORY'S BLACKEST HOUR

I've never known you do a wrong thing
Never ever before
God how could you
So declare war?

This day, Tuesday, August the Sixteenth
You took our idol - plus
The shame, you took
Elvis from us!

From that blackest hour on
History will seek revenge
She'll gather all Elvis's fans
Presley's death will avenge!

Enemy now after Centuries
You'd better run oh Sire,
You knew you were
Playing with fire!

Fans'll never rest again, for into
His death they'll probe and prod
The world's declared
War, on you God

... Say your prayers, God!

TRIANGLE

A guitar, a song,
A "Wiggly" leg!
A young man offered a world
And the fans would beg

A quite handsome guy,
With the dark handsome looks
This was the guy - "*The*" Guy - that
Filled movies and books

That guitar took him
A long long long way
His popularity soared
"*The Man*" of his day!

Girls screeched after him,
Boys and men admired
Of their uncrowned King,
Loyal public *never* tired

Elvis alone gave
Birth to Rock 'n' Roll
A "Wiggly" leg, a guitar,
And he had "a Ball"!

That "Ball" carried on
A Stardom life through,
Oh Elvis how *could* this world
Be the end of you?

KING-SIZE STAR

There was a star in America
That shone and glistened as a gem
Audiences of millions
He sure could "hold" them

Presence he had in abundance,
Best compliment of all
Was, millions copied their King
And entered "The Ball"

Now that Star is "over" them
But they're not over him
His magnetism clinging
In death, his Stardom's never grown dim

Now it is Nineteen-<u>Ninety-Nine</u>
And by gosh Elvis you live on,
This year has Millenium Eve
Is calling - a "Wanted One"

It's as though a sacred being
Did awaken a world so deep
Rock 'n' Roll's King-and-President
Now they won't let you sleep!

Tears impossible to dry
Elvis blew a world - "Sky-High".

EVERY ONE A GIGGLE

Not long to wait - then it
Came - "The Famous Wiggle"
My, the silly thrill of it all
Every one a giggle!

That Giant of a King
Snapped a public from "forlorn"
Consequences, being a world went
Mad, when Rock 'n' Roll was born

An Army snapped *him* up too, I
Wonder how he did adjust?
But march that path he went
Salute "the others" he must!

Not a moment's lonesome
For the girls he had an eye,
And they surely swamped him for a
Souvenir - this "Wow" of a guy!

King of a certain style,
And there ain't no "If's" or "Buts"
For pioneer of Rock 'n' Roll I give
Ten-out-of-ten for his guts!

His own man always, a
Guitar alone his boss,
In later years Elvis remained
The "Fun Kid" he always was!

DARES AND DAREN'TS

He *dared* to give it a go
The Rock 'n' Roll he borne,

And the mighty oak trees grow
From the tiny acorn

Give up was something he *daren't*
E'en for his public's sake,

When he sang - "*Are you lonesome tonight?*"
Then this my night would make!

There are some good impersonators
And some are sloppy too,

But Elvis nonetheless your fans
Do *dare* to copy you!

Into the Army he was called
So Elvis *daren't* refuse,

And no way would I *dare* to
"*Step on his blue suede shoes*"

"Taking America by storm
So a Rock 'n' Roll was born."

ELVIS'S ANIMAL KINGDOM

For you Elvis
We'll be as the crocodile
- And try a big smile,

To
Elvis
Presley
Zoo

And tho' we fret
We'll be as the elephant
- And never forget

Our enthusiasm,
High as the eye of the giraffe,
- Is not just in spasm

We'd return you
With the speed of the cheetah
- To take us from our "blue"

For you awaits
The mighty hug of the bear
- So El, get on your skates!

The Majesty of King of beasts,
The gentility of the lamb,
All are descriptive of our El
Who hit the world with a wham!

"Elvis your Rock 'n' Roll Zoo
Will never ever
Forget to remember
You!"

EMOTIONS

We could conjure up a host of "mushiness",
Yet it all would be sincere,
Elvis if sentiment would return you
And bring you back here

If oceans of our tears, would swim you right back,
Or the breeze sweep you up to
Land you safely on the world's stage again,
Smiling would be true

If loving could hold you and admiration,
If God could bear your absence,
Or if the guilt of our missing you would
Sure rid my conscience

Our sad sighs treble, and only for you is
Our tidal wave of passion
Deepest of feelings for you Elvis won't ever
Go out of fashion

"Emotions
Of magic potions."

NINETEEN-SEVENTY-SEVEN

Naughty, naughty year
Nineteen-Seventy-Seven,
You grabbed our Stars
And sent them up to Heaven

Year of Queen's Jubilee
We were robbed of Presley,
Crosby - and - Charlie
Year you behaved quite fiercely!

Deaths of Elvis, Bing'n'
Lovable Charlie Chaplin
The two to sing'n'
Charlie kept us laughin'

Now to Heaven this
Trio of bright Stars are borne
Left their "Heaven" down here
To take a Heaven by storm

Seven is lucky
Or so we are told,
This time it's meant disaster
As the year did unfold.

MARSHMALLOW DREAM

Elvis now you may continue
In your tranquil, serene,
Warm and cosy,
Marshmallow dream

Pink, soft, fluffy
Elvis's marshmallow dream,
An Elvis Presley passing was
Harsh, shallow, mean!

In God's world he's
Now to take tuition
We'll recall that his dream sure came
To fruition

We must break up
'Cos the party's over,
We'll pass his message how once he
Lived in clover

The "Big-Fame" swell
Reduced now to "Puffy"
We are reminded now how dreams are
Only fluffy

"All dreams must end
my friend."

HOPE YOU DON'T MIND

A little apprehensive
As to your feelings
Elvis, that I've put you in a book
Hope you don't mind you're in my dealings?

I have enjoyed the work,
I've tried to be kind,
Many people do write books -
I sincerely hope you do not mind?

I'll take comfort
In this common touch,
I just hope
You don't mind too much?

It is but a simple book
Containing poems
In its pages, and it is *my* hope
In this way *you'll* land in many homes.

PEN IS ALMOST DRY

It has worked so hard
My pen - to do you credit
Elvis I feel its strain on
My book to edit

Keeping warm and flowing
My pen - has carried on in
Staying faithful to you amid
The havoc and din

Like me it can't stop
Not minding how long it took
My loyal pen, tho' flagging,
Kept up through my book

My pen and me, well
We neither can lay idle,
Are honouring this our debt
We owe our idol

It won't let us down,
Unaware me it's bailing,
My pen is on its last legs
I sense it's failing

Understand El, please
My pen says, "Whisper Goodbye"
Forgive us both El for the
Pen is almost dry.

DIVIDED

Presley!
Introduction of Rock 'n' Roll
Oh Elvis how so true -
- Divided we fall!

Elvis!
What on earth could have meant
It was *one* thing we could not blame
On the Government

You know!
This dividing was God's alone
Only He could call - "Time"
And so called you "Home"

This world!
Left to swallow the bitter pill
Is really up in arms
And aghast at this chill

Minus!
You now King, Rock 'n' Roll will roll
For you really started
Something in the soul

It's thanks!
To your parents from all of us
Of the Angels up there
Now El, - we're envious!

PUTTING DOWN MY PEN

Putting down on paper
All his name stood for,
There're not enough words
As we open dictionary's door

Putting down on paper
His main beneficiary,
Thus is the daughter
Of our Elvis Presley

Putting down on paper
What is in my heart,
Why oh why did the
King have to part?

Putting down on paper
A man among men
Elvis, I've written much of you
Now I must put down my pen

The heartbreak, the sadness, the tears
I've really gone to town
The kisses for a King of years
Putting them all down.

GOODBYE

Elvis now it's "Final Goodbye Time"
And I definitely am signing off,
But just like you took up all my life
So you have taken up my Book-of-Love

My poems have been easy, your death hard,
Now both come to their conclusions here now
I dry my tears' oceans once'n for all
For to see you take that sad final bow

There's no sentiment I've left uncovered
Living on in a glory there are but few
Your "Don' wanna be Tiger" and your "Teddy-Bear",
Plus your "Blue-Suede-Shoes" are awaiting you

You're leaving many "Weeping Willows" El,
Throughout a whole world there's not a dry eye
I am merely just another fan
My pal, buddy, brother - Goodnight, Goodbye

Goodbye from a world.

HAVE WE FORGOT?

Have we Elvis
In our selfish "Blue"
Oh the shame
Have we forgot to thank you

Elvis, oh please
Forgive our manners,
Been wrapped up
Carrying sadness banners

A Universe in
Many ways you shook
I salute
And thank you, for filling up my book

Self-pity trips us
Strips us of our graces
When we lose our famous
The longer our faces

- Thank you Elvis Presley.